Super, Spectacular Pearlie

Pearlie in Central Park

D1396136

WENDY HARMER

Illustrated by Gypsy Taylor

RANDOM HOUSE AUSTRALIA

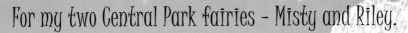

For my two Central Park fairies – Misty and Riley.

A Random House book
Published by Penguin Random House Australia Pty Ltd
Level 3, 100 Pacific Highway, North Sydney NSW 2060
www.penguin.com.au

 Penguin
Random House
Australia

The works in this collection were originally published separately by
Random House Australia in 2010–2016
Super, Spectacular Pearlie first published by Random House Australia in 2018

National Library of Australia Cataloguing-in-Publication data available.

ISBN 978 0 14378 676 4

Cover and internal illustrations by Gypsy Taylor
except confetti stars © Lami Ka/Shutterstock
Cover design by Penguin Random House Australia
Internal design and typesetting by Kirby Armstrong,
Jobi Murphy and Kate Barraclough
Initial series design by Jobi Murphy
Printed in China by RR Donnelley
Asia Printing Solutions Limited

It was a crisp winter morning and Pearlie was riding high in the sky on Queen Emerald's magic ladybird. Her home was far, far away. Down below, she could see the whole of Central Park, New York City.

'Hurly-burly!' cried Pearlie. 'This place is huge! Crystal must be the busiest fairy ever.'

As she flew closer, Pearlie was amazed to see that everything was covered in sparkling snow. She had heard about snow, but it had never fallen in Jubilee Park.

'Frost and icicles!' exclaimed Pearlie. 'How beautiful!'

Queen Emerald herself had arranged for Pearlie to stay with Crystal the Central Park Fairy for a wonderful winter holiday. The ladybird landed on a deep snowdrift and watched as Pearlie took her map and set off to find Cherry Hill.

From across an icy lake Pearlie spotted a magnificent black and gold fountain.

'Oooh! There's Crystal's place!' she cried.

She hurried towards it and was surprised to see that right on the tippy top, sitting on a round glass lamp, was a small furry creature. It had the cutest face ever, handsome whiskers and a large bushy tail.

It was one of the famous grey squirrels of Central Park.

'Hiya! I'm Chester,' he called. 'You must be Pearlie. We've been waiting for you.'

'Hello there,' said Pearlie.

'It's real kind of you to look after the park while Crystal's away on her vacation,' Chester smiled.

'Pardon?' gasped Pearlie. 'I thought I would be staying with Crystal. Isn't she here?'

'Dang!' said Chester. 'There must be some mistake. Crystal's flown off to Hawaii. But she asked me to give you this.'

Chester gave Pearlie a note, and this is what it said:

Queen Emerald's ladybird flew off at once with the news.

An icy wind blew through Central Park. Pearlie pulled her coat tightly about her as big fat snowflakes swirled through the air and fell on her head.

'Brrrr ...' Pearlie shivered. 'How will I ever manage? I've never looked after a park this big before.'

'Now, don't you fuss,' said Chester. 'Me and my buddies will help. You better come on in before you turn into a purple popsicle!'

Chester leapt from the fountain, scurried along a bare branch and disappeared through a hole in the trunk of an old oak tree.

Pearlie picked up her suitcase and flew after him. Through the hole and down, down, down she fluttered in the dark until she landed with a 'bump' on the floor of the squirrels' den.

Pearlie dusted off her coat and saw four big eyes staring at her.

'Say "howdy" to my friends Misty and Maple,' said Chester.

'We know all about you, Pearlie,' Maple sweetly cooed. 'Why, you're as pretty as a picture.'

Pearlie blushed madly.

'You're just in time,' said Misty. 'Please share our supper.'

Misty put a small walnut on the table and the three squirrels eyed it hungrily. It didn't seem enough for everyone.

'The snow came early this year,' explained Chester. 'I wish we'd stored more nuts and acorns to last the long winter.'

'We might find a morsel or two buried under the ice and snow,' Maple added. 'And when spring comes, there will be flower buds to nibble.'

'I hope the season changes real soon,' sighed Misty. 'I'm famished!'

Pearlie felt sad for the squirrels. They did look awfully thin and spring seemed a long way off.

'I have some rose petal muffins in my bag,' she said. 'I made them myself. Would you like to share?'

'Yes, please!' cheered the squirrels.

They held the muffins in their delicate paws and munched happily.

When the squirrels' tummies were full, they chattered to Pearlie about this and that and then settled down to sleep in a soft and furry heap.

But Pearlie was wide awake. Even if she was
a stranger in Central Park, she had to help her
new friends! She would see to it first thing in
the morning.

Pearlie was up at dawn. She watched as the squirrels dug busily through the snowdrifts and found nothing to eat at all.

Suddenly, Pearlie heard squawking. She peered through the frosty bushes and saw a crowd of birds noisily pecking at a feeder filled to the top with delicious sunflower seeds.

As she flew closer the birds spied her with glittering eyes.

'Caw, caw! Who are YOU?' the birds screeched. 'Go away!'

'Excuse me,' said Pearlie politely. 'Can you spare any seeds for some starving squirrels?'

'GET LOST!' the nasty birds shouted. 'This food is for US!'

They flapped their wings and swiped at Pearlie with their claws. Pearlie dodged their cruel, sharp beaks and flew to a nearby tree.

How could she get those selfish creatures to share their food? Even if she zapped the birds with her wand, she still wouldn't be able to get the seeds out. The opening was simply too small for a fairy to squeeze through.

And then Pearlie had a very good idea.

She flew down to the snow-covered grass and called to the squirrels.

'Chester, Misty, Maple!'

When they had all gathered, she told them her plan.

'Just like the birds, we'll sing for our supper,' explained Pearlie. 'We'll put on a show. It's what we do back home in Jubilee Park. Let's go!'

The three squirrels clapped their paws and
bounded after Pearlie, their bushy tails twitching
with excitement.

That afternoon, when the birds of Central Park flew over Cherry Hill, their beady eyes spied a poster on a tree trunk.

THE
★AMAZING!★
THE
★AWESOME!★
Squirrels
on ICE!!
COME ONE, COME ALL
DONATION: Sunflower seeds

A blue jay, who was the greediest of all the birds, cackled with laughter.

'Squirrels can't skate!' he shrieked at Pearlie. 'I'm not paying one good seed until I see those fur balls twirl!'

Now Pearlie was more determined than ever to convince the birds to give their sunflower seeds to see the show. All afternoon she watched Chester, Maple and Misty practise their skating moves on the ice-filled fountain. She helped them up whenever they landed with a furry THUD!

Later, when the sun had disappeared behind dark clouds, the lamps on the Cherry Hill fountain glowed brightly.

The jays, the woodpeckers, the wrens and the finches crowded on every branch. They were twittering with curiosity.

Pearlie had used her magic to decorate the golden flowers and bluestone bowls of the fountain with frozen spider webs. Icy dewdrops shone like diamonds in the lamplight.

But Chester was nervous. 'Can we do it, Pearlie?' he asked.

'Yes we can!' Pearlie declared.

Her wand flashed and beautiful music wafted through the freezing night air.

Misty and Maple appeared in shimmering costumes. They sped across the ice paw in paw, waltzing and looping around each other with amazing grace.

The fat blue jay fell off his perch in surprise and bounced on the ice. 'Awwk!'

'Tweet, tweet! Chirp, chirp! Go Misty! Go Maple!' the other birds whooped in wonder.

Then came Chester in a bow tie and top hat. He leapt and spun like a champion using his bushy tail to steady himself. Double ... then triple axels! A super-duper falling leaf flip with extra nuts!

'Ooooh!' The crowd was simply astonished. 'More, more!' they squawked. 'WHAT A SQUIRREL! WHAT A SHOW! ENCORE!'

This was better than anything ever seen in the bright lights of Broadway!

Chester whizzed around the fountain one more time. He jumped high, high into the air. The birds put their wings over their eyes. They could not watch. Then Chester landed back upon the ice ... and a terrible CRACK! echoed through the park.

Chester's back feet went right through the ice. SPLASH! He was in the freezing water. The birds flapped away in fright, dropping their sunflower seeds as they went.

'Heeelllppp!' called Chester.

'Snowflakes and blizzards!' shouted Pearlie. She whizzed to the icy puddle and offered her wand to help poor Chester out.

Then Pearlie was astonished to find another wand next to hers. She turned to see a fairy dressed warmly in red, white and blue.

It was Crystal the Central Park Fairy!

Between them both, Pearlie and Crystal dragged poor Chester from the freezing depths.

'Phew!' said Chester.

'Yahoo!' yelled Crystal. 'You fell through because the ice is melting, Chester. That means that spring is on its way at last!'

'Way to go!' shouted Misty and Maple as they danced about and gathered the dropped sunflower seeds.

'My stars!' laughed Pearlie.

That night in the squirrels' cosy den, Pearlie and Crystal cooked up a feast of sunflower seed soup, soufflé, donuts and pretzels!

When the squirrels were fast asleep, the two park fairies had a serious talk.

'I can't figure out how the mix-up happened,' said Crystal. 'But as soon as Queen Emerald's ladybird told me I was needed, I flew home as fast as I could.'

'I'm so sorry you had to leave sunny Hawaii,' said Pearlie.

'Are you kidding?' Crystal chuckled. 'I can vacation any time, but there's no finer place to be than Central Park in spring!'

Sure enough, the next morning was fine and sunny and the first shoots of green grass could be seen through the snow.

As the days passed, Crystal and the squirrels showed Pearlie all the wonders of Central Park. She was thrilled to see the buds burst into blossom on every tree.

'Twirly-whirly!' sang Pearlie as she flitted from flower to flower.

'You go, girlfriend!' cheered Crystal.

All too soon it *was* time for Pearlie to go.

Chester, Misty and Maple made an archway
with their furry tails and Pearlie ducked under it.

'We'll miss you like crazy,' said Crystal. She gave
Pearlie a mighty hug.

'And I'll miss you too,' replied Pearlie. 'I'll never
forget Central Park, New York City.'

With a flash of jewelled wings Queen Emerald's ladybird took to the sky with Pearlie aboard. She was looking forward to her next adventure.

Pearlie often visited Central Park in her dreams.
She saw herself curled up in the warm squirrel
den as the snowflakes drifted in silent beauty
around the bare branches of the old oak tree.

Super, Spectacular Pearlie

Pearlie and the Cherry Blossom Fairy

WENDY HARMER

Illustrated by Gypsy Taylor

RANDOM HOUSE AUSTRALIA

For Maevie, my very own cherry blossom

It was springtime in Japan when Pearlie the
Park Fairy flew over the old city of Kyoto,
and the famous cherry trees were in bloom.

'Buds and blossoms! Everything is pink,'
Pearlie sighed happily. 'The whole of this park
is perfectly pink!'

When Pearlie was named 'Fairy of the Year', she had left her home in Jubilee Park to visit all the other Park Fairies in the world. What a life it must be, she thought, to live here in the flowering cherry trees of Japan!

She waved goodbye to Queen Emerald's magic ladybird and it flew off through clouds of rosy petals.

'Konichiwa!'

Pearlie turned to see an elegant fairy dressed
in a gloriously embroidered silk gown.

'My name is Akiko,' she said as she bowed low.
'Welcome to the Park of the Imperial Palace.
Will you have some tea?'

'Yes, please,' Pearlie replied.

Akiko lived in an old lantern carved from stone.
Its roof was covered in soft green moss.

'Oooh, it's lovely,' said Pearlie.

'It's very cosy when the snow comes,' Akiko
smiled. 'Please leave your boots by the door.'
Pearlie was very pleased she had worn her
best frilly socks!

She sat at a low table and Akiko served
a delicious breakfast of tiny sugary cakes
and a bowl of hot green tea.

'Thank you,' said Pearlie.

'In Japan we say "*arigato*",' said Akiko.

Everything sounded very strange to Pearlie.
She had never met a Japanese fairy before,
and had so many questions to ask. She learned
that Akiko's lovely dress was called a '*kimono*'
and that '*konichiwa*' meant 'hello'.

'My job is to care for all the cherry trees – the *sakura* – in the park,' said Akiko. 'I sing to them and let them know spring is coming. It's very important that the *sakura* make a lovely display.'

Pearlie nodded. At home in Jubilee Park she was always very proud when the roses looked their best.

'Soon the park will be crowded with visitors who come to see the flowers,' said Akiko. 'And my home is the perfect place to watch all the parties from without being seen.'

Pearlie and Akiko peeked out of the old stone lantern. All morning families and friends came by to spread picnic blankets under the trees. They ate, played games, strolled by the pond and took lots of photographs of the branches heavy with blossoms.

'Everyone in Kyoto loves cherry blossom time!' declared Akiko.

'Look!' cried Pearlie as she pointed with her wand. 'That flower is moving all by itself.'

Akiko giggled. 'Hee, hee! That's a paper umbrella and under it is my friend Yuki. He is helping himself to the picnic treats.'

Pearlie looked again, and sure enough, there was a mouse carrying away a whole tea cake.

'I hope Yuki's hungry,' laughed Pearlie. 'That's a whopping cake for a very small mouse!'

Rumble!

The two fairies were startled to hear thunder.
The sun disappeared behind towers of black
clouds.

'It's a spring storm!' shouted Akiko. Pearlie
pulled her wings tightly around her. She didn't
like storms. In the next moment, huge hailstones
came smashing down.

All over the park the visitors grabbed their picnic
blankets and their bats and balls. They ran for
the gates as fast as their legs could go.

'*Tasukete kudasai!*' they shrieked.

'They're calling for help,' cried Akiko over the
deafening noise of hailstones on the roof
of the lantern.

"Aiee, aieee!" came a terrified voice.

Pearlie and Akiko looked out and there was Yuki! He was holding his paper umbrella and being blown high into the sky. Giant balls of ice battered the cherry trees. The wind howled and the air was filled with swirling petals.

Bang!

A mighty hailstone hit the roof of the old stone lantern.

Crack!

Suddenly it was split right down the middle! Huge hailstones pelted onto the floor and a freezing wind whipped through the lantern. Pearlie and Akiko gripped the edge of the front door and watched as Akiko's kimonos and furniture were all picked up and whisked away, out of sight.

'Hurly-burly!' shouted Pearlie.

And then, just as quickly as it had started, the storm stopped.

The sun peeped out from behind the clouds and Pearlie and Akiko looked out from their hiding place. They were amazed to see that every single cherry tree was as bare as could be! All the blossoms had been torn from the branches and were lying in a thick pink carpet on the ground.

'This is terrible!' wailed Akiko. 'And where is my friend Yuki?'

'Aiee, aieeee!' the voice came again.

Pearlie spotted a tiny figure clinging to the roof of the Imperial Palace. 'There he is!' exclaimed Pearlie. 'We'll go and help him. Quickly, let's find our wands.'

But Pearlie and Akiko could not find them. The lantern was perfectly bare. Their wands had been blown away across the park, along with everything else.

'We'll have to fly Yuki down instead' said Pearlie, and she whizzed off with a very soggy Akiko after her.

High up on top of the palace roof, Yuki the mouse was shaking with fright. 'Eeek, eek,' he squealed. 'Please help me!'

Akiko held Yuki's shivering paw. 'This is my new friend Pearlie,' she said. 'We will get you down.'

'Take our hands!' said Pearlie.

The two fairies tried very hard to lift Yuki, but sadly, the little mouse had eaten one too many tea cakes. He was just too heavy!

'Eeeyah!' sobbed Yuki.

'What will we do now?' wailed Akiko.

Then Pearlie had a very good idea. 'You go and find Yuki's umbrella,' she said to Akiko. 'I've got work to do.'

Pearlie flew down to the grass and began
to pick up the fallen cherry blossom petals.
It was hard work without her wand, but
soon enough she had pushed them
into a great big pile.

'YUKI! WAIT UNTIL A BREEZE
COMES, HOLD YOUR UMBRELLA
HIGH, AND THEN ...
JUMP!' Pearlie called.

Just then a soft wind sang through the branches of the cherry trees.

'NOW!' shouted Pearlie.

Yuki leapt from the roof holding his paper umbrella. It was a bit ragged from the storm, but still strong enough to hold him. The breeze blew Yuki this way and that. Down and down he floated with Akiko flying close behind.

WHUMP!

Yuki landed safely in the soft pink petals.

'Hooray!' cried Akiko as she clapped her tiny hands.

Yuki climbed from the petals and bowed very low. '*Arigato*, honourable friend Pearlie,' he squeaked. 'How may I assist you?'

'Well,' Pearlie replied thoughtfully, 'could you help us find our wands?'

'*Hai!*' agreed Yuki and he scurried off.

Akiko looked at her broken lantern. 'I'll have to find a new place to live,' she said sadly.

'There are so many lovely lanterns in the park,' said Pearlie. 'It might be fun to have a new house for the spring and summer.'

'Why, yes it would,' agreed Akiko.

Pearlie and Akiko spent the afternoon house-hunting in the Imperial Park. They looked at many, *many* lanterns. Some were made of stone and others of paper. Some were too roomy and others too small.

Then they spied a beautiful wooden one painted as red as cherries.

'Oooh, it's perfect!' said Akiko.

At that moment, Yuki came scampering across the scattered pink petals. He held a precious fairy wand in each paw.

Pearlie and Akiko were very glad to see them. 'Thank you! *Arigato!*' they cheered.

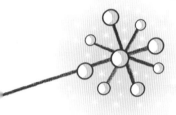 

Yuki bowed once more, very pleased to have been of service. 'I saw all of Akiko's furniture too,' he puffed. 'But I'm afraid all her pretty kimonos landed in the pond and have been nibbled by the golden carp.'

'Fish and frocks!' gasped Pearlie.

'Hee, hee, hee,' giggled Akiko. 'It does not matter. I can surely make new ones.'

Pearlie zoomed off to look for Akiko's furniture. She found her bed in a bush and her teapot up a tree! Pearlie was thrilled and used her magic to zap Akiko's belongings into her new home.

Akiko got to work too. The clever little fairy gathered an armful of petals and found her sewing kit full of pins and needles and beautiful silk threads.

That evening in the lovely new lantern, Pearlie and Akiko feasted on blossom buns, petal sushi and cherry fizz that Yuki had made.

Then Akiko modelled her petal *kimonos*, all handmade in shades from deepest rose to snowy white. She had collected moss and leaves to make shawls and wide *obi* belts.

'You are the prettiest fairy in all Japan,' sighed Pearlie.

'*Hai!*' Yuki agreed.

In the days that followed, Pearlie met all the creatures that lived in the Imperial Park. She rode on the backs of the tortoises, swam with the golden carp and played hide-and-seek with the dragonflies.

When the cherry trees were at last covered in bright new leaves, Pearlie knew it was time for her to go. Queen Emerald's ladybird soon arrived to take her away.

Akiko offered Pearlie a small gift tied with scarlet ribbon. 'I will never forget you,' she said. 'Every time the cherry trees are covered with buds, I will think of Pearlie the Park Fairy.'

'And I will think of you too,' said Pearlie. 'When spring comes to Jubilee Park and the golden flowers burst on the wattle trees, I'll remember cherry blossom time in Japan.'

Pearlie bowed to her new friends.

'*Sayonara!*' said Akiko and Yuki. 'That means "goodbye".'

'But not forever,' said Pearlie as she kissed them both.

Pearlie jumped on board the ladybird and it took to the sky. She heard Akiko's voice calling through the bare branches: 'Nothing is forever. Not even the famous cherry blossoms of Kyoto.'

Pearlie unwrapped her gift and found a small pearl that had been gathered from an oyster shell in the Imperial Pond. She sniffed back a little tear and then she smiled – she was off, looking forward to her next adventure.

SUPER, Spectacular Pearlie

Pearlie and the Silver Fern Fairy

WENDY HARMER

Illustrated by Gypsy Taylor

RANDOM HOUSE AUSTRALIA

For Shirley, our own precious Kiwi.

Pearlie the Park Fairy flew through a long, white cloud. Below her was the beautiful country of New Zealand.

Riding on the back of Queen Emerald's magic ladybird, Pearlie saw huge snowy mountains, shimmering lakes and a mighty green rainforest.

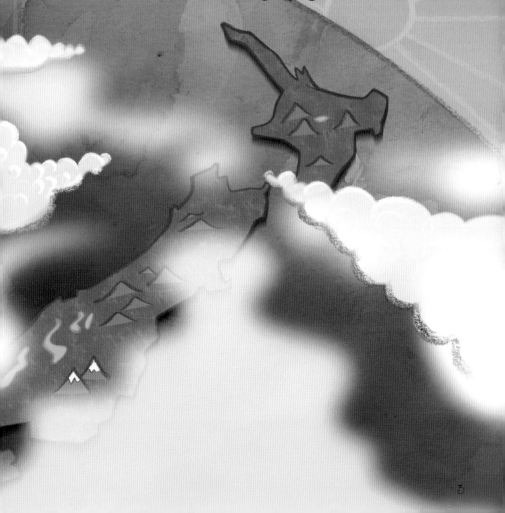

The ladybird flew lower through the
towering trees and set Pearlie down
on a mossy rock, then it winked and
whizzed off. It was a cool misty
morning and Pearlie wrapped a
warm coat over her wings.

'Hurly-burly!' she said. 'I've never
seen a park like this before.'

Pearlie heard a voice tinkling like a silver bell. She darted to the bank of a rushing stream and there was a beautiful fairy riding in a little canoe made from a seed pod. The fairy was wearing a long, feathery cloak.

She smiled and waved to Pearlie. *'Kia ora!*
Welcome! Jump in and start paddling.'

Pearlie thought it was rather curious that they
were taking a canoe instead of flying, but she
leapt in and off they sailed.

'My name is Omaka,' said the fairy. 'In Māori talk that means "place where the stream flows".'

'Are you a park fairy too?' asked Pearlie.

'Āe mārika! Yes, indeed!' smiled Omaka. 'But we're a long way from the city here in the ancient rainforest. This is a park for nature at its wild and most beautiful best.'

The little canoe slipped downstream around rocks and under low branches. The sunlight sparkled on the damp fern fronds, turning them silver.

Pearlie thought she'd never seen a sight so lovely.

Soon the bubbling stream joined another that was moving more swiftly. Pearlie looked up in alarm. Ahead was a waterfall tumbling down a rocky cliff. The little canoe was heading straight for the swirling water!

'Reeds and ripples!' cried Pearlie.

'Hold on. Paddle harder!' called Omaka.

The canoe twirled and danced and swayed on the water. Then, with barely a splash, it sailed right through the waterfall and beyond, into a cave twinkling with lights.

'Ooooh, stars and moonbeams!' said Pearlie.

'No, they're glow-worms,' laughed Omaka.
'They're showing us the way to my place.'

Before long, the fairies were sitting on gleaming paua shells in Omaka's cosy cave house and sipping on snowberry tea.

'It was a good day to come,' said Omaka. 'I'm planning a little birthday supper for my friend tonight, and you'll be able to meet everyone. I have to bake the cake and deliver these invitations.'

'I'd be glad to help,' said Pearlie.

'*Ka pai!* Excellent!' said Omaka. 'I've put a list of the guests and a map of where to find them in this bag.'

Pearlie took the small woven bag and slung it over her shoulder. 'And who is celebrating their birthday?' she asked.

'My friend the tuatara,' Omaka smiled. Pearlie had never heard of such a creature. 'He's one hundred and fifty years old today.'

'One hundred and fifty years old!' Pearlie
gasped.

'Yes! That's a lot of candles and a very big cake,
so I'd better get started,' said Omaka. 'And so
had you, Pearlie. *Mā te wā.* See you later.'

Pearlie climbed back in the canoe and set off.
The paddling made her very warm and she took
off her coat. Her silvery wings fluttered free.

Pearlie followed the map deep into the rainforest. She tied the canoe to a reed and read the name on the first invitation. It was 'Colin the kiwi'.

'Roots and twigs! What's a kiwi?' wondered Pearlie.

She flitted off and quickly spotted a small brown hairy bundle sitting in a hole in the ground.

Pearlie flew down and saw two bright eyes staring at her through bristling whiskers at the top of a long, narrow beak. So a kiwi was a very large bird!

'How do you do, Colin?' said Pearlie politely. 'Here's a party invitation for you.'

'Wonderful,' Colin snorted happily.

'If you could fly by at sunset, that would be perfect,' said Pearlie.

'Well, of course I can't fly, but I'll wander along just the same,' he said. '*Tēnā koe*. Thank you!'

Pearlie was puzzled. A bird that couldn't fly? She didn't want to be rude and ask what was wrong with his wings, so she simply thanked Colin and flew off.

The next invitation was for 'Hoki the kakapo'.

'Oh dear,' said Pearlie. 'I've never heard of a kakapo either.' Was it a fish or a frog, or another odd kind of creature, she wondered.

Just where the map said, Pearlie spied a big lump covered in glorious green feathers snoozing under a tree fern.

So a kakapo was a bird too!

It was much bigger than the kiwi. In fact, it was the most enormous parrot Pearlie had ever seen. She gently woke Hoki and handed over the invitation.

'Please fly by later for some cake,' she said.

'Well, I've never been one for flying,' yawned Hoki as he fluffed his feathers. 'But I do love cake, so I'll hike along the trail and see you there.'

Now Pearlie was a little worried. Another bird that wouldn't fly? Why ever not? She fluttered lower than before, just to be careful. This was a strange part of the world indeed!

Now Pearlie had one last invitation to deliver, for 'Wanda the short-tailed bat'.

'Well, at least I know what a bat is,' said Pearlie as she flew along. 'She will be hanging upside down in this tree here.'

But there was no bat in the branches.

Then Pearlie saw something moving down on the forest floor. A small snout was poking out from under a leaf. Pearlie's wings flashed as she zoomed down.

'Wanda?' asked Pearlie. 'Is that you?'

The leaf stirred and out came a tiny snuffling bat.

'Āna. It's me,' said Wanda.

Pearlie gave her the invitation. 'Just fly on over
when the sun has gone down.'

'I'd rather stroll by, if it's all the same to you,' said Wanda.

'Why, yes, of course,' said Pearlie kindly, even though by now she was beginning to feel rather nervous. She looked towards the treetops. Why was nobody flying?

Pearlie ran off through the forest as fast as she could. She didn't dare use her wings. There must be something up in the sky that would catch any creature that flew. Maybe it would eat her!

The sun was fading and scary shadows crowded the forest. Pearlie found a hollow in the roots of a tree and huddled there for a moment. Her tiny heart was beating fast.

'Beaks and claws!' said Pearlie. 'I'd better be careful and walk back to Omaka's place, even though it will take me ages. And . . . brrr,' She shivered. 'It's getting c-c-cold.' She pulled her coat over her shoulders.

Suddenly a huge head topped with fearsome spikes poked itself in front of Pearlie's face. Two great black eyes stared at her!

'Eeeek!' she cried. 'Don't eat me! Please, don't eat me!'

Pearlie felt for her wand and then remembered she had left it behind in the glow-worm cave.

The scaly beast opened its mouth wide. Surely it would eat Pearlie with one mighty gulp!

Then the great mouth smiled.

'Heh, heh! Don't be frightened, little one. I'm Grandfather Tuatara. Can I offer you a lift to Omaka's cave? It's my birthday today and I hear there will be cake!'

Pearlie laughed with surprise. 'You're a lizard,' she said.

'*Nāhea!* Not me!' chuckled Grandfather Tuatara. 'I come from the dinosaurs who roamed the earth 200 million years ago. This is the only place on earth you can find me. Climb up and I'll tell you a few stories along the way. Watch out though, my name means "peaks on the back" in Māori.'

Pearlie scrambled aboard, minding the spikes on Grandfather's back, and they set off. No one in Jubilee Park would ever believe she'd ridden a dinosaur!

As they rambled along, crunching over carpets
of leaves and ducking under dripping fern fronds,
Grandfather Tuatara told Pearlie many tales of
ancient days. He pointed out tiny flowers, plants
and moss on the forest floor. Walking was a
good way to see them all.

'There are so many creatures here that don't fly. Why is that, Grandfather?' asked Pearlie.

'Well, long ago, the forest was safe and we had no need to fly, so many creatures never learned how,' Grandfather explained as he trudged along on sturdy legs. 'But since then many things have come across the ocean that can hunt and hurt us. Humans brought creatures with sharp teeth – rats and cats, dogs and possums, weasels, stoats and ferrets. We couldn't fly away to escape. In my time I have seen so many good friends disappear,' he sighed sadly.

Pearlie was quiet, thinking about all the poor creatures in danger. What would happen if the fairies were to disappear too?

'We hope for better times,' said Grandfather.
'I know that young humans care about
us and that's a very good thing.'

'It is,' Pearlie agreed.

'*Rā whānau ki a koe!*
Happy birthday to you!'

Grandfather Tuatara stopped in his tracks. In a clearing were all his friends – Omaka, Colin, Hoki and Wanda – and in the middle was a tremendous birthday cake with one hundred and fifty candles.

Pearlie leapt from Grandfather's back. As she jumped, her coat fell off.

It was then that Omaka spied Pearlie's beautiful wings. 'You can fly!' she cried.

Pearlie was astonished to see that Omaka had no wings at all.

A fairy that couldn't fly? She was just as precious as all the other creatures of the ancient rainforest.

'Can you light Grandfather's candles for us?' asked Omaka, as she gave Pearlie her wand.

'Of course!' said Pearlie. She whizzed around the cake, lighting all the candles in a blinding flash.

Grandfather Tuatara took a deep breath and blew them all out.

'We have a present for you, Pearlie,' said Omaka. 'It's a koru carved from greenstone. It is the shape of a new fern frond, which brings new life and hope. Wear it to keep you strong.'

'I will keep it forever,' said Pearlie. 'And I hope all my friends in the rainforest will live in peace.'

'*Ehara ehara*, indeed,' said Grandfather. 'Now it's time for cake!'

Super, Spectacular Pearlie

Pearlie in Paris

WENDY HARMER

Illustrated by Gypsy Taylor

RANDOM HOUSE AUSTRALIA

For Mlle Claudia, the fashionista!

It was springtime in Paris! From high on Queen Emerald's magic ladybird, Pearlie could see many grand buildings, the Eiffel Tower, and beautiful parks bursting with fresh flowers.

'Hurly-burly!' sang Pearlie. She was thrilled to be visiting one of the world's loveliest cities when it was at its prettiest.

'There's the *Jardin du Palais Royal*!' she called
to the ladybird. 'That's where Fifi the Fairy lives.
In a palace! Imagine that!'

The ladybird darted through the royal grounds, the magnificent gardens and set Pearlie down in a bed of bright yellow and pink tulips.

From behind a bloom, out jumped a small fairy.

She tapped one tiny toe.

'*Enfin!*' she said in a cross voice. 'At last!'

Pearlie smiled and said, 'Hello, my name is –'

'You do not speak French?' asked the fairy.

'No, I'm afraid not,' Pearlie replied.

'*Zut alors!*' muttered the fairy. 'You are late and you do not speak French. This is too, too bad! It is just as well that you are very pretty. Follow me. *Tout de suite!*'

The little fairy zoomed away. 'That means "at once"!' she called over her shoulder.

The fairy flitted along a palace terrace and then landed in front of a small door at the foot of a grand stone staircase.

Pearlie quickly followed. She wondered if this could be the famous Fifi? She wasn't very friendly.

Once inside, Pearlie was amazed to see a long hall lit by splendid crystal chandeliers.

'Twirly-whirly,' sighed Pearlie. 'How beautiful.'

The little fairy handed Pearlie a lovely
ruffled gown.

'Take off those plain clothes and old boots and
put this on *immediatement!*' she ordered. 'My
other models are already dressed.'

How rude, thought Pearlie. Her own dress
was pretty enough and her boots were
almost brand new.

'There must be some mistake,' she said. 'I'm not
a model.'

'But why not?' said the fairy. 'Your hair is
magnifique!'

'Why, thank you very much,' Pearlie blushed.
'But, may I ask, are you Fifi?'

'*Oui!*' said the fairy as she smoothed her dark
hair. 'The most famous fairy in all of Paris!'

'Well, I'm Pearlie the Park Fairy and I've come to
visit from Jubilee Park.'

'Oh, *excuse moi!*' exclaimed Fifi. She then kissed Pearlie, not once, but three times, as the French like to do. 'I forgot you were coming! You see, I have been so busy with my spring collection.'

Pearlie wasn't exactly sure what a 'spring collection' was, although she knew it wasn't like the cake crumbs the ants collected from picnics on the sunny lawns of Jubilee Park.

Fifi opened a wardrobe. Inside were many more fabulous shimmering gowns.

'It is my fashion for the new season. I sew them from the petals of French lilies, roses, iris and sprigs of rosemary,' said Fifi proudly.

'I make my own clothes, too,' said Pearlie. 'I have some here in my bag. Would you like to see them?'

'Er … *non*,' Fifi sniffed. 'No time. You will have a little tea and a sweet cake and then I will show you how clothes are *properly* made in *belle Paris*.'

Soon Pearlie was sitting in a fancy chair sipping a delicious cup of rosehip tea and nibbling on an almond macaron.

'You will be truly amazed,' said Fifi. She clapped her hands and from a doorway came tall and lovely fairies who paraded up and down the carpet, one by one.

They wore long glittering gowns, flowing capes and the most extraordinary feathered hats. Their dainty high-heeled slippers were covered with tiny jewels.

Pearlie *was* amazed. 'Stitches and sequins!' she gasped.

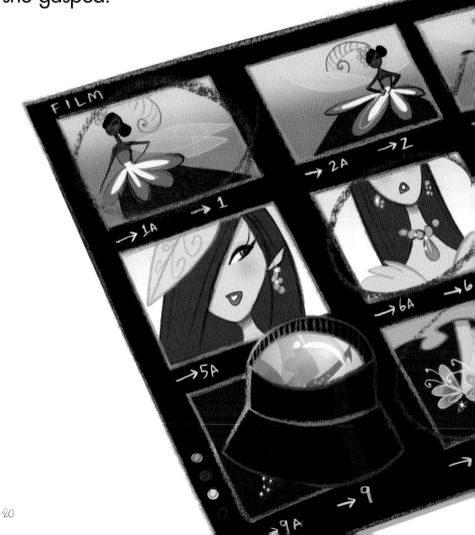

They were hardly the sort of clothes Pearlie would wear to work in Jubilee Park when she was hanging dewdrops in the spider webs.

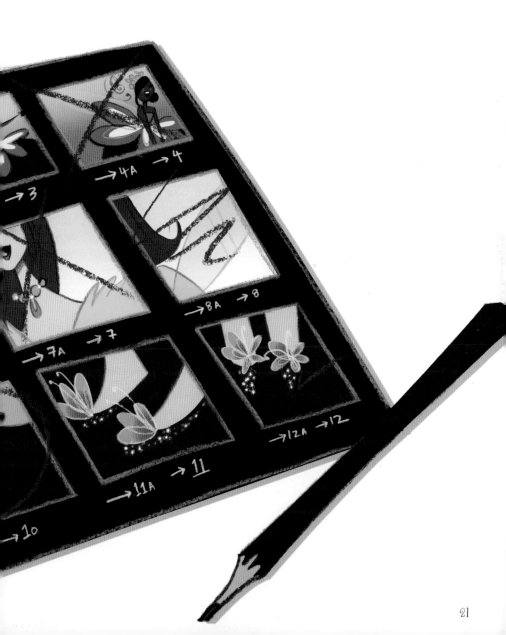

It was late when the parade finished and Fifi showed Pearlie to her charming *boudoir*. (That's the French word for a lady's bedroom.)

'Sleep well,' said Fifi. 'Tomorrow everyone is coming for the parade and it will be a very busy day. *Bonsoir*. Goodnight.'

Under the stairs of the Palais Royal, Pearlie slept soundly.

At dawn she was woken by a terrible shout.

Pearlie flew out of bed and found Fifi on the floor in front of her wardrobe. Her beautiful clothes were now little more than scraps of leaves, petals and a few feathers and sequins. The sad pile was covered in silver slime.

'Roots and twigs!' said Pearlie. 'What happened?'

'Someone left my front door open last night and all my beautiful clothes – *toutes mes belles robes* – have been EATEN!' Fifi cried.

'Who would do such a thing?' asked Pearlie.

'It is the work of *escargot*! SNAILS!' Fifi threw
herself into a chair and wept loudly. 'All the
fine fairies of Paris will soon be here to see my
collection! What will I have to show for all my
hard work? *C'est un catastrophe!*' she cried.

Pearlie knew that if there were no clothes
for the fashion parade, the day would indeed
be a catastrophe.

Poor Fifi, thought Pearlie.

She immediately set to work and followed
the silver snail trail out the door and through
the tulip beds.

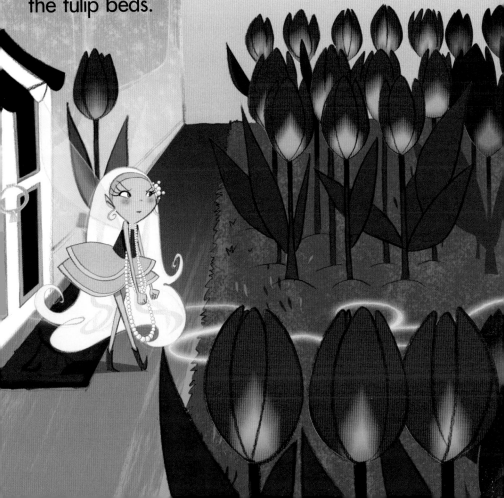

'AARGH! GROAN!'

The sound was being made by a fat snail, who was looking very unhappy.

He was the guilty one, all right! In fact, he still had a bit of sleeve hanging out of his mouth.

'Aha!' said Pearlie. 'I hope you had a fine feast, you greedy thing.'

'OOOH!' moaned the snail.

Pearlie felt sorry for him. He really did not look well.

'Can I get you something? I'm Pearlie, what's your name?' she said, hoping he spoke English.

'Percy,' he replied. 'EERGH! A small cup of water, if you please.'

Pearlie fetched the water and when Percy had drunk it, he felt up to telling his tale.

'Two days ago I came from my home in London across the English Channel by mistake in a box of spinach,' he said sadly. 'When the vegetables were delivered to the palace kitchen, I spied the chef. Do you know they EAT snails in Paris? They serve us with garlic butter!'

'Hurly-burly!' said Pearlie. 'How dreadful!'

'I was lucky to make my escape,' Percy said with a shudder.

'So what happened last night?' Pearlie asked.

'I was lost and wandering the garden when I smelled a beautiful aroma. It was like a dream. I followed the scent and was soon having the most delicious dinner I have ever eaten, until something went down the wrong way.'

'I imagine it was a sequin,' sighed Pearlie. 'They're very hard to digest.'

'BURP! Yes they are,' said Percy.

Pearlie then informed Percy of exactly what he had done. He had dined out on all of Fifi's finery.

'Good gracious,' he said. 'How truly ghastly of me.'

Percy agreed to find Fifi and explain everything

'*Je suis désolé*. I'm *so* sorry.' Percy felt so guilty he apologised to Fifi in French *and* English.

But Fifi was still mad.

'You can't blame him,' said Pearlie. 'Snails do have very poor eyesight.'

'Your spring collection was five stars!' said Percy.
'Apart from … BURP!'

Up came a sequin which landed at Fifi's feet.

Fifi's face turned a dull shade of green. 'Eergh!
I make fashion, not fine food,' she wailed. 'What
will my models wear? I must show *something!*'

Then Pearlie had an idea.

'The models can borrow my new spring clothes!'
she said. 'They're made from wattle, lilly pilly and
kangaroo paw.'

Fifi wrinkled her tiny nose. 'You make your
clothes from the feet of *kangourou? Non!* This
will not do. Not at all.'

'No,' laughed Pearlie. 'They're all native
Australian flowers. I reckon no-one here has
ever seen them before.'

'Hmm,' said Fifi. 'That could be something very, very new. Show me what you have and perhaps I can make a quick alteration with a bow or a sequin … *çà et là* … here and there?'

Soon Pearlie and Fifi were sitting with their heads together and their sewing needles flashing.

Later that afternoon, the chandeliers sparkled on a glamorous gathering of the fashionista fairies of Paris. Some had flown in from London and New York!

They were looking forward to the delights Fifi had to offer.

Pearlie sprinkled fairy dust perfumed with spring flowers from back home in Jubilee Park.

'Ooh, la, la!' the fairies exclaimed.

Percy appeared as the Snail of Ceremonies.
(After all, he spoke two languages.)

'*Mesdames et Messieurs*, Ladies and Gentlemen,'
he said. '*Bienvenue!* Welcome!'

The lights dimmed and the show began. Fifi was
very nervous, but Pearlie held her hand tightly.

It was a dazzling parade!

The crowd went wild to see bright fluffy balls of yellow wattle, purple lilly pilly berries, the blazing red of desert flowers and the glowing colours of the kangaroo paw.

All of Pearlie's dresses had been given that special 'Fifi' touch and looked *magnifique*!

When the lights came up, the audience stood and clapped wildly.

'Superb! Extraordinaire! Awesome!' they cheered.

Fifi and Pearlie took a bow together and kissed one another's cheeks – not once, twice, three, but *four* times.

'Merci, Pearlie. Thank you,' said Fifi. 'With your help, once again I am the toast of Paris. You and Monsieur Snail are to be my guests here at the Palais Royal for as long as you would like.'

45

Pearlie and Percy had an excellent time seeing all the sights. Pearlie flew to the top of the Eiffel Tower and Percy slid all the way up (which, it must be admitted, did take a week, but Pearlie didn't mind).

When spring was over it was time for Pearlie to leave, although Percy wanted to stay forever. Fifi said he was very welcome to stay and that she would make sure he wasn't eaten for supper.

Pearlie was sad to leave Paris but she was delighted with the lovely gowns Fifi gave her.

She could just imagine herself fluttering though Jubilee Park at dawn, glittering in French sequins from the top of her feathery hat to the toes of her jewelled slippers.

'I'll always remember Paris in the springtime,' she sighed.

'*Au revoir*,' Pearlie called softly. 'Goodbye!'

Super, Spectacular Pearlie

Pearlie and the Flamenco Fairy

WENDY HARMER

Illustrated by Gypsy Taylor

RANDOM HOUSE AUSTRALIA

For my very own dark-eyed Señorita, Miss Helen xxx.

It was a bright and beautiful afternoon when
Pearlie flew into sunny Spain.

From the back of Queen Emerald's magic
ladybird she had a wonderful view of the plazas,
fountains and the royal palace in the lovely old
city of Madrid.

She spotted the patch of green that was the
Real Jardín Botánico.

'Hurly-burly! There it is,' she exclaimed. 'That's
the Royal Botanic Garden where Florentina lives.'

The ladybird set Pearlie down at the feet of a
large statue and flew away.

Suddenly, from behind a bush, out jumped a fairy with long dark hair, sparkling brown eyes and a swirling scarlet skirt.

'*Hola*, Señorita Pearlie!' she cried. She tapped the tips of her shoes on the stone path, twirled, clicked her fingers and shouted, '*Olé!*'

Pearlie clicked her fingers too and shouted back,
'Hooray!'

The two new friends hugged each other.

'I have a wonderful surprise for you!' Florentina said happily. 'I hope you brought your *zapatos de baile*.'

'Pardon?' said Pearlie.

'Your dancing shoes.' Florentina smiled.
'Tonight I am giving a special party in your
honour. A dance party! And everyone will be
there to meet you.'

Now, Pearlie had her boots and her slippers with her, but she had not brought any dancing shoes.

Pearlie could sing and fly like a bird. Everyone said so. But as for dancing?

Pearlie's cheeks turned bright pink. 'Um, I'm not very good at …' she started to say.

Florentina beamed at Pearlie, spun on her heels and said, '*No hay problema!*'

Florentina picked up Pearlie's bag
and tap-tapped away along the
path. Pearlie followed, wondering
what would happen when all of
Spain saw that she had two left feet.

Soon the fairies came to a
wonderful shady pergola.

Fairy Florentina rummaged in her bag and handed Pearlie a pair of shiny black shoes.

'Here, put these on,' she said. 'Hurry. Señor Philippe will be here *en un momento*.'

As Pearlie buckled on Florentina's shoes, she heard a clicketty-clack, clicketty-clack echoing across the marble floor.

Striding towards her was a tall and handsome fellow. His eyes were big and black, his two long antennae were twitching and he wore a splendid moustache. Two of his six thin legs ended in shiny shoes.

He was a very sleek Spanish cricket!

'It's Señor Philippe,' whispered Florentina. 'He is here to teach us the flamenco!'

'Flamenco? What's that?' asked Pearlie.

'It is the dance of FIRE!' Señor Philippe shouted as he stopped in front of her. 'We stamp our feet and dance for the joy of life! I am here to teach you THE DANCE!'

Pearlie thought that all sounded very nice, but she was a bit tired after her long trip from Jubilee Park.

'Perhaps I could have a cup of tea?' she asked.

'NEVER!' Philippe boomed. 'We are never too tired to dance the flamenco.'

The next moment there was music and a voice
wailing 'Aiyeeee! Aiyeeee!' Pearlie saw a
small beetle bent over a guitar and singing
his heart out.

'Raise your arms like this!' said Florentina.
'Follow me!'

And away she went, madly tapping her toes and fluttering her skirts, just like the frilly petals on a red carnation.

'Twirly-whirly!' gasped Pearlie.

Señor Philippe clapped loudly. 'It is your turn, *señorita*. Go!'

Pearlie stepped out and tried her best to keep in time with the music but soon she had her feet and wings all tangled up.

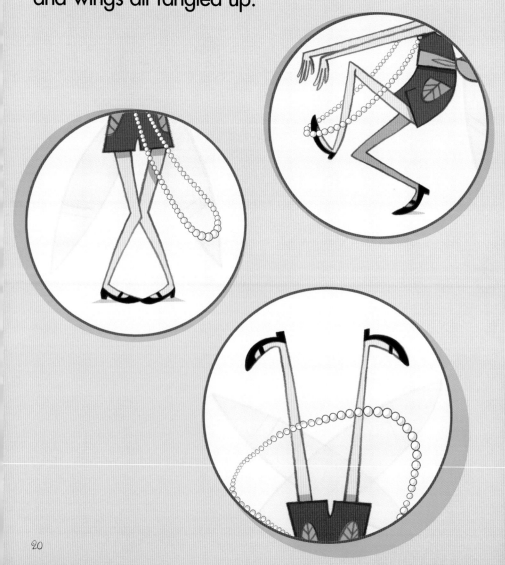

'No, no, no!' said Señor Philippe. '*Otra vez!*
Again!'

All afternoon Pearlie tried her best, but it was
no good.

The more Señor Philippe shouted and the faster
the guitar played, the more she stumbled and
bumbled and thought she might fall over.

It was almost dusk and a big round Spanish
moon was rising when the lesson was over
at last. By now Pearlie was very, very tired.

'You were *magnífico*, my friend,' said Florentina.
'Now, there is time for a rest and when the stars
come out we will go to the dance. Everyone will
be there to meet you.'

Now Pearlie was even more worried. She had
not mastered the flamenco at all, and her poor
feet were tired and throbbing.

Pearlie was glad to sit down as Florentina served a supper of spicy fried potatoes, pickled peppers and slices of olive stuffed with almond.

'We call it tapas. That means lots of little dishes, so you don't get too full to tap your feet,' said Florentina as she poured Pearlie a tall glass of fresh orange juice with cinnamon and honey.

As Pearlie ate every delicious morsel, she almost forgot about her sore feet. Almost. Poor Pearlie would have liked to go to bed and sleep the night away.

But Florentina had been so kind and was so excited. Pearlie must dance the dance of FIRE. *Olé!*

Soon it was time to go. Florentina changed into another beautiful swirling gown covered with lace and frills. It was even more spectacular than the last. Pearlie didn't have anything like it in her bag.

'You can borrow one of mine,' said Florentina.

The dress was black and red and very grand, but somehow didn't quite suit Pearlie who, it must be said, always looked her best in pink.

'Do you mind?' asked Pearlie as she raised her wand.

'*Nada!* Not at all!' laughed Florentina. 'Your dress must be just as you wish.'

With a wave of Pearlie's magic wand, the gown was instantly layers and layers of lovely pink.

'One more thing,' said Florentina, producing her own wand.

It had a red ruby on top, and with one flourish, Pearlie's dress was covered in polka dots. Even her shoes were spotty! On her head she wore a beautiful lace veil and a pink carnation.

'*Maravilloso!*' cried Florentina. 'Let's go dancing!'

'Taps and twirls!' Pearlie wailed. 'I'm really not very good at ...'

But the flighty Florentina had already hurried off and, once again, Pearlie chased after her.

The moon was bright and the stars were twinkling on the fairy flamenco dance. It was an extraordinary sight! All the fairies of Spain were there.

The music was loud and fast. On the white marble dance floor skirts flew as feet tapped ever-faster. The sight of it made Pearlie feel dizzy.

All around them was a clicking noise that sounded like the call of cicadas in summer back home in Jubilee Park.

'They're castanets,' explained Florentina. 'We use them to keep the beat, from our fingers to our feet.'

Then she jumped up and joined the crowd,
snapping her castanets all the way.

Pearlie was watching everything and very much hoping that no-one would ask her to dance, when she saw Señor Philippe coming towards her with his hand outstretched.

'Time for you to show everything you have learned about the flamenco,' he said, smiling through his big moustache. *'Vamos a bailar! Let's dance.'*

Pearlie's heart sank to the floor. But to refuse the invitation from Señor Philippe would be very bad manners indeed. And she did so want to make fairy Florentina happy.

She stood up and ...

… Oh dear!

Pearlie's feet tangled in her long, flowing skirt.

She tripped and fell on her wand.

The top of it broke off with a loud 'snap' and every one of its precious pearls scattered and bounced across the floor.

Boink, boink, boink. Clatter!

'Hurly-burly!' cried Pearlie. What if the pearls got under the feet of the dancers? What if they skidded and fell over?

That would be awful.

In a flash, Pearlie went after her shiny pearls.
She darted this way and that between the feet
of the fairy dancers.

She flew up and down and round about. One by
one, she scooped the pearls from the floor and
held them in her tiny hand.

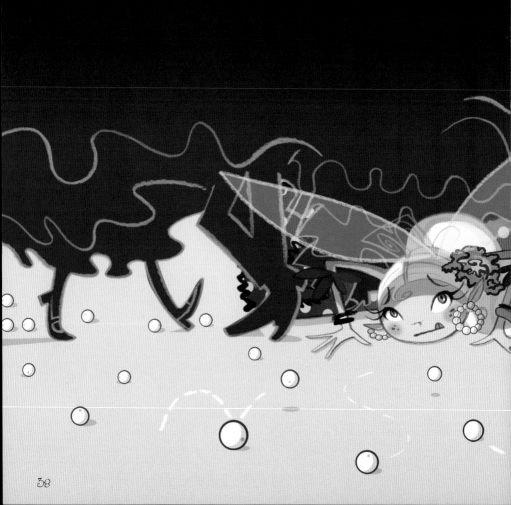

'Click, clack,' they rattled, like pearly castanets.

She darted this way and that, finding one pearl and then another.

One, two, three, four, five, six … She almost had them all.

Then Pearlie saw from the corner of her eye that the Spanish fairies were hurrying from the dance floor.

They stood and watched in amazement as Pearlie whirled and twirled in the air. Her wings flashed in the moonlight and her spotty skirts tossed and tumbled.

Seven, eight, nine … Stars and moonbeams!

At last she had them all.

Then all the Spanish fairies began to stamp their feet, clap their hands and shout: *'Olé! Olé! Olé!'*

Señor Philippe was astounded.

'*Estupendo! Magnífico!*' he said. 'Never have
I seen the flamenco danced quite like this,
Señorita Pearlie.'

'*Bien hecho.* Well done!' laughed fairy Florentina.
'You certainly showed everyone here a thing
or two.'

Pearlie was very pleased. She blushed the same colour as the flower in her hair.

But there was still the problem of her broken wand and her handful of pearls.

'*Lo siento*. I'm so sorry,' Florentina said sweetly. 'But we will have your wand fixed as soon as we can. *Rápidamente!* Until then, please use my red ruby wand for your stay here in Spain. It has special powers, as you will see.'

And do you know? That red ruby wand *was* very special.

Everywhere Pearlie went in the gardens of Spain, she only had to wave it and all the flowers would ruffle their petals, sing and dance for her.

It was the most magical summer ever.

When the petals on the flowers began to fall, it was time for Pearlie to leave. Señorita Florentina presented Pearlie with her own wand, fixed and good as new.

'Always remember, Pearlie,' she said. 'Everyone can dance. One must always dance like no-one is watching. The flamenco comes straight from the heart and you have a very big heart.'

Pearlie vowed to always remember what
Florentina had said.

And as she flew up and away from the gardens
of Spain, her heart was tapping a wild and
wonderful flamenco beat.

SUPER, Spectacular, Pearlie

Pearlie Goes to RIO

WENDY HARMER

Illustrated by Gypsy Taylor

RANDOM HOUSE AUSTRALIA

For Miss Maeve — growing her wings
and becoming a beautiful butterfly.
I love to watch you flutter!

It was a hot and steamy morning when Pearlie the Park Fairy looked out over the wonderful city of Rio de Janeiro.

Queen Emerald's magic ladybird had dropped Pearlie off on the top of a mountain near the city. From there the view almost took her breath away.

'Hurly-burly!' gasped Pearlie.

Away in the distance she could see beautiful beaches with tumbling surf. A little closer were the jumbled white buildings of Rio. And right below her were valleys of deep green rainforest.

4

'*Vista maravilhosa!*' said a voice behind her.
'Yes! It is a truly marvellous sight.'

Pearlie turned around to see a fairy with a wide smile. She was shading herself with a huge flower umbrella.

'I'm Morena,' said the fairy, as she tossed her shiny black curls. 'And you must be Pearlie. *Bem vinda!* Welcome to Brazil.'

'Why, thank you,' said Pearlie. 'I'm so pleased to be visiting your park.'

Then Pearlie shaded her eyes from the burning sun and looked about.

'Where *is* your park, exactly?' she asked.

'You're in it right now,' laughed Morena.
'Tijuca Forest. This is one of the biggest parks
in the world! Now follow me.'

8

Morena fluttered her lovely wings and zoomed
down, down into the leafy forest. The tiny fairy
was very fast. She dodged huge tree trunks,
bright flowers and even flew under a waterfall.

Pearlie was right behind her.

At last Morena came to a clearing. She pushed aside heavy leaves and thick vines and led Pearlie into a cool, quiet hollow.

'Oooh, it is lovely here,' said Pearlie.

A bright orange beetle scuttled in with a tray of drinks and snacks.

'There is lime or melon juice and *baba de moça* cake. It's made from coconut milk and cream.' Morena said sweetly. 'Eat and drink, Pearlie. You have come to Tijuca Forest just in time for the most exciting night of your life!'

Pearlie nibbled at the cakes and sipped her juice
as Morena told her story.

'The Butterfly Carnival will begin soon and all
the butterflies will parade through the forest.
It is *muito bonito*. That means very beautiful,'
said Morena.

How exciting! Pearlie adored butterflies.
Back home in Jubilee Park she loved to watch
them dance and twirl among the flowers.
And, she had to admit, their wings
were often prettier than her own.

As the afternoon went on, Morena told tales of the strange creatures that could be found in the old forests of Brazil.

There were lizards that walked on water. Bats of the night that ate fish. Massive spiders with stripes like tigers. And even a fish that ate underwater trees!

Pearlie had never heard anything like it.
She was amazed.

'You've travelled a long way,' smiled Morena.
'The sun is going down now, so let's both
sleep. Whatever noises you hear in the night,
remember you are safe with Morena of Tijuca.'

The fairy flitted off and Pearlie fell asleep in a soft bed of moss.

It was still dark when Pearlie was woken by strange sounds she had never heard before.

SWOOSH, SCRABBLE, SNUFFLE, SCRATCH!

The Tijuca rainforest was full of creatures that loved the hot and steamy night.

Pearlie lay awake until the first light of dawn crept into her room. The orange beetle brought her some delicious caramel tarts.

But she wasn't the only one having breakfast.

MUNCH! MUNCH! MUNCH! MUNCH!

'Roots and twigs! What's that sound?'
said Pearlie.

Fairy Morena appeared. '*Bom dia*. Good
morning. That noise is not roots and twigs . . .
it's leaves. It's the caterpillars, and they are very
hungry. Come with me and you will see.' MUNCH!
MUNCH!
MUNCH!
MUNCH!

The two fairies set off.

It was an astonishing sight. Before them was a huge bush. Caterpillars of all shapes and colours covered every leaf. Some had spikes on their backs. Some were covered in feathery spines. Others had long, curly antennae.

And every single one was eating great holes in the green leaves. The caterpillars seemed to be getting fatter by the minute.

'*Caramba!* I have so much to prepare for the carnival. Could you please look after the caterpillars for me today, Pearlie?' asked Morena.

'Of course,' said Pearlie.

'*Obrigada.* Thank you,' said Morena as she flew off. She called over her shoulder, 'And watch out for the hungry birds!'

Pearlie looked about. She could see many beady, birdy eyes in the forest above. The naughty birds were all hoping to make a meal of the caterpillars.

If they did, there would be no butterfly parade.

'Shoo, go away!' called Pearlie. She flitted this way and that, using her wand to zap any bright tail feathers and beaks she could spy.

'AWK, AWK, AWK!' The birds squawked in fright and flapped away through the forest.

Pearlie was very busy all day long.

Not only did the pesky birds keep coming back, but as the caterpillars grew they shed their skins and dropped their old clothes all over the place. Pearlie picked them up and folded them neatly.

The noise of the caterpillars chewing through the leaves was deafening. All day it got louder . . . and louder.

MUNCH, MUNCH, MUNCH, MUNCH!!!

'Phew!' said Pearlie as her wings drooped.
'I do hope they all turn into butterflies soon.'

One by one, the caterpillars stopped eating. They crawled to the underside of the bare branches, where they were safe from the hungry birds. They shed their skins for the very last time.

When Morena returned that evening, all the caterpillars were quiet. They were busy making themselves chrysalises. Inside each chrysalis, a caterpillar would turn into a butterfly.

'Finalmente! Finally we will have some peace,' said Morena. 'Now we can prepare our costumes for the carnival. They must be *espetaculares*!'

'Yes,' laughed Pearlie. 'Spectacular.'

The days passed quickly as Pearlie and Morena watched over the chrysalises. They collected feathers and flowers from the forest to make their headdresses, skirts and sandals.

Then Pearlie had a bright idea.

'I think I will use those old caterpillar skins to make a wonderful cloak,' she said.

Morena agreed that would be a very special costume and sure to catch the eye.

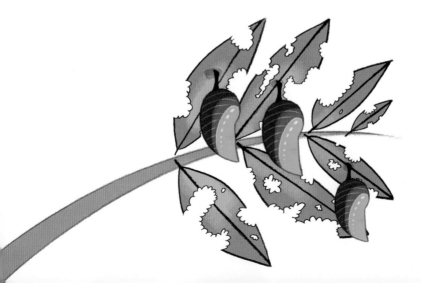

After much sewing, the bright and beautiful cloak was ready. Pearlie put it on and stepped out of the shade to show Morena.

Pearlie twirled and said, 'How do I loo–'

In an instant, a great big greedy parrot swooped down from the branches. It thought Pearlie was a delicious caterpillar treat.

It whisked Pearlie off in its beak and darted through the rainforest.

'EEEEEK,' screeched Pearlie.

In a flash, Morena flew after the hungry bird.

'*Para, para!* Stop, stop!' she shouted.

But the parrot would not stop. Up and up it
flew to the top of the mountain and beyond.
Right up into the cloudless blue sky.

'Help, help!' cried Pearlie.

What could she do? Her wand was tucked in
her bag back at the clearing. The parrot's fierce
beak was crushing her wings. Just one gulp
and she would be gone. Swallowed like a tasty
caramel tart!

ZAP!

Morena's wand gave the parrot's tail feathers a mighty sting.

SQUAAAAAAWWK!

The parrot's beak opened and out fell Pearlie.
But her wings were crushed and she could not fly.

Down, down from the sky and through the rainforest she tumbled. Past trees. Over waterfalls.

'Huuuuuuuurly-buuuuuuurly!' cried Pearlie.

She was sure to fall on the rocks below.

WHUMP!

Pearlie landed with a bounce on a shimmering . . .
What was it? A flying carpet?

When Pearlie caught her breath, she saw she
had fallen on top of butterfly wings.

A great swarm of baby butterflies had hatched
and flown up the mountain to her rescue.

'*Obrigado*, Miss Pearlie!' they whispered. 'Thank you for looking after us when we were caterpillars!'

'No, no. Thank you,' gasped Pearlie.

The butterflies dropped her gently onto a flower and sang, '*De nada!*' Then they flew off giggling to find a supper of sweet nectar.

'That means "no trouble at all",' said Morena, who was happy to find Pearlie safe and sound. She shuffled her tiny feet.

'You're dancing!' laughed Pearlie.

'It's the samba. The favourite dance of Rio!'
Morena replied as she wiggled some more.
'The butterflies are getting ready, and we will
all be doing the samba at the Butterfly Carnival
tonight.'

That evening, as the sun dropped behind the
mountain and the forest fell dark, Pearlie and
her new friend admired each other's costumes.
They both looked *fantásticas* – although Pearlie
had wisely decided to leave her caterpillar
cloak behind.

'It is time for the famous Butterfly Carnival
of Tijuca to begin,' called Morena.

She waved her wand and a million fairy
lights sparkled. A swarm of glittering beetles
banged on drums, fat frogs croaked in a
booming chorus and the whole rainforest
swayed to the samba beat.

Next came a twirling, whirling parade of butterflies. Their wings glowed like brilliant jewels.

In all her life Pearlie had never seen a sight so wonderful.

'This is the best night ever!' she shouted as she danced to the rhythm.

'*Um beijo!* I give you a kiss, dear friend,' said Morena.

'*Muito bom!* Very good,' laughed Pearlie.

Then the little two fairies held hands and danced the night away in the magical rainforest of Tijuca.

SUPER, SPECTACULAR Pearlie

Pearlie and the Imperial Princess

WENDY HARMER

Illustrated by Gypsy Taylor

RANDOM HOUSE AUSTRALIA

For my father Graham Frederick Brown,
who inspired my love of reading.

It was an icy cold winter's morning when Pearlie flew over the old city of Beijing.

She had been invited to the Imperial Garden of the Forbidden City to celebrate Chinese New Year with a fairy princess. It all sounded very grand.

From on top of Queen
Emerald's magic ladybird,
Pearlie could see the
magnificent palace below.

'Hurly-burly! It's
splendid!' she gasped.

Pearlie guided the ladybird to fly through the massive Gate of Supreme Harmony.

The ladybird set Pearlie down and flew away.

Just then, someone called, '*Zǒng suàn!* At last, you're here!'

Pearlie looked up and saw a very pretty, tiny face.

She flitted up the steps with her suitcase and waited patiently for the beautiful big red and golden doors to open.

'Ooh,' said Pearlie to herself, 'I've never been to a New Year's party in a place as magnificent as this.'

The doors opened and there stood a fairy dressed in very fine clothes.

'My name is Princess Li Mei, which means beautiful plum blossom,' she said.

'Oh, what a lovely name,' Pearlie replied. 'And I'm . . .'

The princess snapped her fingers. '*Gǎn kuài!* Hurry up. Snow is coming.'

And with that, Princess Li Mei turned on her heel and disappeared inside.

All Pearlie could do was hurry after, dragging her suitcase behind her.

Behind the wall was Li Mei's private pavilion. It looked just like a jewel box! Its roof was topped with little figures of lions, birds and dragons.

Pearlie could not believe her eyes as she walked from room to room. Inside the pavilion was a palace too.

The lanterns, chairs and couches were covered
with embroidered amber silk.

Pearlie thought of her little shell on the top of an
old stone fountain in Jubilee Park and her one,
very messy, room. She wondered what Princess
Li Mei would say if she saw it.

But the princess had disappeared. Surely she should have offered Pearlie morning tea after her very long trip.

Pearlie spotted a long table covered with lots of pretty dishes filled with cakes and sweets. Everything looked delicious!

She had piled a plate with tasty treats when
Princess Li Mei came back.

'*Heng!* These are not for you,' she scolded.
'My cook made them for the party tonight.'

'Oops, sorry,' said Pearlie. She blushed bright pink.

The princess handed Pearlie a broom, a duster and polishing rags. 'My pavilion must be carefully cleaned from top to bottom. It can't be done on New Year's Day or all my riches will be swept away.'

'But . . . but,' said Pearlie. 'I'm not very good at housework.'

'Then it is just as well I have only 20 rooms. There are 9000 in the Forbidden City,' said the princess, before she vanished once more.

'Roots and twigs!' said Pearlie. 'That princess is the rudest and bossiest fairy I've ever met.'

Still, Pearlie's invitation *had* promised a huge party, a lion dance, Chinese opera and then fireworks. Even though she was weary, she was happy to help out with preparations.

Pearlie sighed a tiny sigh and got to work sweeping the enormous banquet hall.

KNOCK KNOCK

Late in the afternoon there was a knock at the front door of the pavilion.

Princess Li Mei swept into the hall wearing a shimmering red gown. Her long black hair was topped with a royal jewelled headdress.

'It must be my first guest. Much too early,' the princess said crossly. 'Well, open the door!' she ordered.

But instead of a guest in party clothes, there was
a young fairy who bowed and said, '*Duìbùqǐ.*
I'm so sorry, princess. I'm the maid. I went to the
wrong place.'

Princess Li Mei turned to Pearlie and shouted,
'Well, if you are not my maid, WHO ARE YOU?'

'I'm a Park Fairy too,' Pearlie explained.

Li Mei scowled. '*Wăn'ān*. Goodnight.
My honoured guests will be here soon.'

'But you sent me an invitation!' Pearlie cried.

'You are mistaken too. Show me!' demanded
Li Mei.

The princess's face turned very red. 'It is my
naughty twin sister Li Wei who has invited you.
Not me.'

DEAR PEARLIE,

PLEASE BE MY VERY HONOURED
GUEST AT A GLITTERING PARTY
TO CELEBRATE CHINESE NEW
YEAR. I HOPE YOU WILL ENJOY
THE LION DANCE, CHINESE
OPERA AND FIREWORKS.

LOVE
Li WEI
和平

Pearlie took another look at the invitation.
Uh oh! It did say 'Princess Li Wei'.

'There is another New Year party in the
Forbidden City tonight?' asked Pearlie.

'Yes! And MINE will be the best,' replied Princess Li Mei.

Then she rudely pushed Pearlie out the door and slammed it shut.

Pearlie pulled out her map and saw there were TWO pavilions in the Imperial Garden.

Pearlie was in the west in the Pavilion of Ten Thousand Autumns.

She should have been in the east at the Pavilion of Ten Thousand Springs!

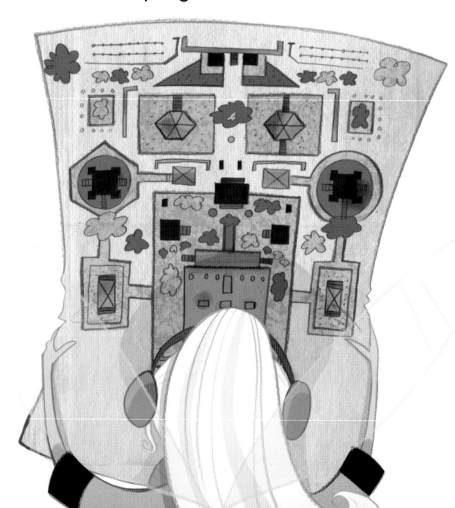

'I must have had the map upside down,' she
wailed. 'Hurly-burly! I have to go.'

'And tell my sister she is NOT forgiven!' Princess
Li Mei yelled through the door.

Oh dear! The two princesses were having a
dreadful argument.

Pearlie wondered what it could be about.

It was snowing in the Forbidden City and the moon was brand new. It was just a silvery slice in the sky.

'Stars and moonbeams! It's so beautiful,' sighed Pearlie. She fluttered here and there, taking in the sights.

As she flew over the vast roof of the Hall of Imperial Peace, something shimmering in the snowflakes caught Pearlie's eye.

What was it?

She took a closer look and found a delicate
ruby necklace draped around the neck of a
small, carved beastie. It must have been lost.

Pearlie popped it around her neck for safekeeping.
She would try to find its owner as soon as she
had the chance.

She flew off and, just as her map said, there was another red and yellow pavilion.

'It's exactly the same as the other one,' said Pearlie in amazement.

Pearlie knocked on the door and it was opened by a fairy who was the image of Princess Li Mei.

'*Huānyíng!* Welcome,' the fairy laughed.

'Gung Hay Fat Choy!' Pearlie said brightly.

She had been practising how to say 'Happy New Year' in Chinese ever since she'd left Jubilee Park.

'I'm Princess Li Wei, which means beautiful rose. And you must be Pearlie. *Ai ya!* Where have you been?'

'I'm sorry I'm so late. I got lost,' Pearlie apologised.

'Come in out of the cold, you must be hungry and tired,' Princess Li Wei said kindly.

Inside, the New Year party was in full swing. All the guests were in wonderful costumes and feasting on dumplings and sticky cakes.

'Buds and blossoms, what fun!' said Pearlie.

Pearlie was shown to a room where she could get dressed for the party. It was charming. The silk cover on the bed looked like a spring garden.

Princess Li Wei sighed. 'I wish my sister was here to celebrate. We always used to sing together for our guests in times gone by.'

'Can I help?' Pearlie kindly asked.

'I don't think so.' The princess shook her head sadly.

Then Li Wei noticed something.

'What is that around your neck, Pearlie?' the princess asked.

'I found it on the roof of the Hall of Imperial Peace,' Pearlie replied. 'Do you know who lost it?'

'*Wā!* It was ME,' gasped the princess. 'It's our mother's ruby necklace! The Jewel of Harmony! I dropped it and could never find it. My sister says that I stole it. But I did not.'

'Then we must go and show her, right now,' said Pearlie. 'I'm sure she will forgive you.'

The two fairies flew off straight away.

The Pavilion of Ten Thousand Autumns was quiet and dark when the fairies arrived. There was no party inside.

Princess Li Wei knocked on the door and called, 'Sister! It is me!'

Princess Li Mei came to the door. She was wearing her dressing gown, ready for bed.

'Zǒu kāi! Go away!' Princess Li Mei said crossly.
'There is no party here. You stole my guests
AND our mother's necklace!'

Princess Li Wei held up the Jewel of Harmony.

'It has been found by our new friend Pearlie.
I lost it, just as I told you,' said Li Wei.

'*Yí!*' exclaimed Li Mei. 'Forgive me, dear sister.'

The two fairy princesses hugged with great joy.

'I am so sorry,' Princess Li Mei sobbed.

'I have missed you,' Princess Li Wei wept too.

Pearlie was so happy to see the sisters in each
other's arms.

'What good luck,' she sniffed. 'Now we should
get to the party. What a surprise for your guests
when they see you together!'

Everyone was amazed when the twin princesses appeared at the party in costumes of the Chinese Opera and began to sing a glorious duet.

They clapped and shouted, '*Tài shénqíle!*
Incredible. Brilliant. Marvellous!'

Pearlie just loved the famous Lion Dance.
She smiled to see all the little fairylings so happy
with their lucky red envelopes full of money.

When everyone was gathered on the balcony for the midnight fireworks, Pearlie gave the guests another surprise.

She flew into the air and used her magic wand to make flowery fireworks! There were explosions of wattle, waratah and kangaroo paw – all her favourites from Jubilee Park.

No one in the Forbidden City had ever seen anything like it.

It was the best party ever!

The two sisters embraced Pearlie and kissed her cheeks. One each.

'*Xièxiè*. Thank you, Pearlie,' sang the princesses together in peace and harmony. 'Gung Hay Fat Choy!'

'And a Happy New Year to one and all!' laughed Pearlie.